# Great-Uncle Dracula

By Jayne Harvey

Illustrated by Abby Carter

A STEPPING STONE BOOK

Random House New York

*To a really "great" grandfather, Robert Lubben*
*—J. H.*

Text copyright © 1992 by Jayne Harvey  Illustrations copyright © 1992 by Abby Carter
All rights reserved under International and Pan-American Copyright Conventions. Published
in the United States by Random House, Inc., New York, and simultaneously in Canada by
Random House of Canada Limited, Toronto.

*Library of Congress Cataloging-in-Publication Data*
Harvey, Jayne. Great-Uncle Dracula / by Jayne Harvey ; illustrated by Abby
Carter.  p.  cm.  "A Stepping Stone book."
Summary: Emily Normal finds it hard enough adjusting to a new town, Transylvania, USA,
populated by vampires, witches, and the like, without the bullying of a third-grade classmate.
ISBN 0-679-82448-0 (pbk.) — ISBN 0-679-92448-5 (lib. bdg.)
[1. Witches—Fiction.  2. Vampires—Fiction.  3. Schools—Fiction.  4. Bullies—Fiction.
5. Moving, Household—Fiction.] I. Carter, Abby, ill.  II. Title.
PZ7.H26755Gr  1992
[Fic]—dc20                                                                                    91-31460

Manufactured in the United States of America   10 9 8 7 6 5 4 3 2 1

# Contents

# ·1·

# Frog Soup

I should have known something was wrong when Great-Uncle Dracula served frog soup for breakfast.

But I didn't. My little brother Elliot, my dad, and I had just moved in with him the night before. Maybe Great-Uncle Dracula didn't know that kids do not eat frog soup for breakfast.

"How do you like your soup, Emily?" Great-Uncle Dracula asked me.

I looked at my bowl of soup. It was dark green. There were green bubbles floating on top. It looked like a project I did for science class last year.

I didn't want to hurt Great-Uncle Dracula's feelings. But I had to tell him the truth. After all, he was going to be making my breakfast from now on. I couldn't possibly eat frog soup every day.

"I'm sorry, Great-Uncle Dracula," I said very politely. "But I always eat toast for breakfast. I don't think I like frog soup."

"*I* like it!" said Elliot.

I couldn't believe my ears—or my eyes. My little brother had already licked every drop of frog soup from his bowl. There were still a few drops of green soup on his lips. Now he stuck out his tongue and slurped those off, too.

"That's disgusting," I said. "How can you eat that stuff?"

"With a spoon!" Elliot said. Then he laughed so hard that his face turned bright red. It almost matched his bright red hair. Elliot is in first grade. He thinks everything he says is hilarious.

Just then my dad came into the kitchen. He

was rubbing his eyes. His hair, which is red like Elliot's, was all messy. He looked very sleepy.

Dad is a writer. Sometimes he stays awake all night writing. That makes him really tired in the mornings.

"Having a nice breakfast?" he asked us.

"I am afraid Emily does not like her breakfast," said Great-Uncle Dracula sadly.

"Why, Emily? What's wrong?" Dad asked me.

"There's frog soup in this bowl," I said.

Dad's face became very pale. "Frog soup?" he said.

"It's delicious!" yelled Elliot.

My dad gave Elliot a funny look. Then he turned to Great-Uncle Dracula.

"Uh, Uncle Drac, do you have a loaf of bread?" he asked.

"Yes, I do," Great-Uncle Dracula answered. "Why?"

"I'd like to make Emily a piece of toast," Dad said.

"Toast? For breakfast? How strange!" said Great-Uncle Dracula. He looked confused.

There is nothing strange about eating toast for breakfast. I should have known something was wrong when Great-Uncle Dracula said that. But I didn't. Maybe nobody ate toast in Transylvania, U.S.A.

Transylvania is the town where Great-Uncle Dracula lives. Now I live here too. I used to live in a town called Plainville. Then my parents got divorced. My dad and Elliot and I moved in with Great-Uncle Dracula so he could help take care of us.

After I finished my toast, it was time to go to school. I'm in third grade. I like school. But today I was nervous. I had no idea what Transylvania Elementary would be like.

I looked at myself in Great-Uncle Dracula's big mirror in the hallway. I have straight reddish hair, like my mom. Today I had it in a ponytail. My glasses were on straight. Good.

I was wearing a brand-new pleated skirt and a matching button-down sweater. All the girls back in Plainville wore skirts and button-down sweaters. I hoped the girls in Transylvania wore them too. I didn't want to look different from everyone else on my first day of school.

Then it was time to leave. Great-Uncle Dracula drove Elliot and me to school in a long black car. It looked like a funeral car. All the other cars on the road were long and black too.

I guess that's when I should have known that something was wrong. But I didn't. Maybe there had been a big sale on long black cars somewhere in Transylvania.

"There it is! Transylvania Elementary School," said Great-Uncle Dracula.

For the second time that day, I could not believe my eyes. The building in front of us didn't look like a school at all. My school in Plainville was made of red bricks and shaped like a big rectangle.

Transylvania Elementary School was very tall. It was made out of gray stone. It looked a lot like a castle.

"Are you sure this is it, Great-Uncle Dracula?" I asked.

"Yes, indeed. It looks the same as it did

when I was a little boy," he said.

I guess I should have known something was wrong by then. But I didn't. Maybe the person who built Transylvania Elementary also liked to build castles.

Kids were lined up in long rows in front of the giant castle door. They were waiting for the first bell to ring. We used to start school that way in Plainville too.

Great-Uncle Dracula pointed to two of the lines.

"That is the first-grade line, Elliot. And over there is the third-grade line, Emily. Line up with the other students. I will tell the school principal you are here."

I walked over to the third-grade line. Things looked very strange to me. I didn't see one button-down sweater.

But I did see that some of the girls were wearing tall black pointy hats and long black skirts. A boy at the front of the line had hair all over his face. He looked just like a werewolf I saw in a movie once. And the boy behind me was very pale, like a ghost. Even his hair was white!

Could it be Halloween? I wondered. No. It was only September. Maybe the kids were dressed up for a play. Our second-grade class in Plainville put on a play last year. I had to dress up like a slice of Swiss cheese.

The girl in front of me in line was wearing a pointy hat. She turned around and smiled at me. She had curly brown hair and green eyes. She seemed nice.

"Hi!" she said. "My name is Winnie. You must be new."

"Yes, I am," I said. "By the way, I like your costume," I added politely.

"What costume?" she asked.

"Your witch costume. You're dressed up like a witch, right?" I said.

"Of course I'm dressed up like a witch. I *am* a witch. Aren't you?" Winnie said.

*That* is when I knew something was wrong.

# ·2·

# Show and Smell

Before I had a chance to answer Winnie's question, the bell rang. It sounded loud and deep and kind of creepy.

In fact, everything about Transylvania Elementary was kind of creepy. I looked around for Great-Uncle Dracula. I wanted him to take me away from this weird school. But I didn't see him anywhere. So I followed Winnie and the rest of the class into Transylvania Elementary.

The inside of my new school looked like a castle too. The halls were dark and dusty.

There were cobwebs everywhere, and spooky shadows along the walls. I kept expecting a monster to jump out of a dark corner and grab me. At Plainville Elementary the walls were bright yellow. The halls were sunny and clean. And there were definitely no monsters hiding in the corners.

I followed Winnie into the third-grade classroom. Everyone scrambled for a seat but me. I waited at the front of the room for the teacher to arrive.

Soon all the kids were sitting down. The teacher must be late, I thought. I looked around the classroom. The desks were the same as the ones in Plainville, but everything else was different. There was a giant skeleton in the corner of the room. There were pictures of bats on one wall. Then I saw a glass tank. Maybe there were gerbils in it. Back in Plainville we had two gerbils in our class, Mike and Ike. But I didn't see any gerbils in this tank. Instead I saw two big hairy spiders! There was a sign over the tank. It said: ICKY AND STICKY, THIRD-GRADE TARANTULAS.

On another wall there was a big poster. GET
READY FOR THE GROSS FACE CONTEST! it said.
I had never heard of a gross face contest before. In Plainville we had a talent contest
every year. Maybe a gross face contest was
something like that.

I was starting to get a little nervous. Where
was the teacher, anyway?

Suddenly a voice behind me said, "You must
be Emily. I'm your teacher, Ms. Vampira."

I jumped a bit. I hadn't even heard her come
into the room.

"Hi," I said as I turned around. Then I almost jumped again.

Ms. Vampira did not look like any teacher
I had ever seen. She was tall and very pale.
Her straight black hair was so long that it
touched her ankles. She was wearing a black
dress.

Ms. Vampira smiled at me. "Class, I'd like
you to meet Emily Normal. She just moved
here from Plainville."

"How come she's called normal? She sure
looks weird to me," said a girl in the back of
the room. She had long straight black hair too.

She was wearing one of those pointy witch hats like Winnie's.

Ms. Vampira frowned. "That's enough, Wanda. I'm sure everyone will do their best to make Emily feel welcome." Then she pointed to an empty desk and said, "Emily, please take the seat next to Winnie Witcherson."

Winnie smiled at me as I sat down, and I felt a little better. But I was still very confused. What was wrong with everybody? Should I ask Ms. Vampira why everyone was dressed up? Was this some kind of joke the school played on new students?

I decided to wait and ask Great-Uncle Dracula about it after school. Ms. Vampira was starting class.

First we said the Pledge of Allegiance. Then Ms. Vampira announced that since it was Thursday, we'd begin with show and smell.

Show and smell? Didn't she mean show and *tell*? Maybe I hadn't heard right.

"Who would like to go first?" asked Ms. Vampira.

The boy who looked like a werewolf raised his hand. "All right, Wolfie," she said. "What do you have for us today?"

Wolfie walked to the front of the room. He had claws on his hands and fuzzy paws for feet.

Wolfie pulled a fancy black bottle from his knapsack. "This is Putrid Perfume," he said. "My aunt Moonerva brews it in her basement. It's her own special blend." Then he pulled the stopper out of the bottle. "Doesn't it smell neat?"

Putrid Perfume smelled worse than skunks and rotten eggs mixed together. It made me choke. The class started to clap for Wolfie, but I didn't. I was too busy holding my nose.

"Thank you, Wolfie," said Ms. Vampira. "Who would like to go next?"

The boy with white hair and white skin raised his hand.

"Okay, Hector. Come up here," said Ms. Vampira.

Hector stood up and walked to the front of the room. He was leading a giant green bug on a leash!

He told us it was a rare Transylvania stink bug. Normally they didn't smell bad, he said. But when you scare them, they squirt stuff that smells really gross.

Hector crouched down and shouted "Boo!" at the bug. A second later there was green slimy stuff all over Ms. Vampira's desk. I held my nose even harder.

Then Wanda raised her hand.

"Ms. Vampira," she said, "the new girl is holding her nose."

Ms. Vampira raised her eyebrows. "Is everything all right, Emily?" she asked me.

I decided to be honest. "Well, actually," I said, "we never had show and smell in Plainville. The Putrid Perfume didn't smell very nice to me. And the stink bug was even worse."

Ms. Vampira thought for a moment. "Your great-uncle Dracula said that things in Transylvania might be a little strange for you. You may hold your nose if you like."

"Thank you," I said.

Hector continued to talk about his stink bug.

Suddenly a strange thing happened. From out of nowhere a note appeared on my desk.

I was kind of scared. I opened the note very slowly. It said: GO BACK TO PLAINVILLE, EMILY *WEIRDO!*

I really wished that I could.

# ·3·

# Scream Cheese and Jelly

Who could have sent me such a horrible note?
I looked around the room.

Winnie saw me look at her and smiled. I
looked at Wanda. She gave me a mean look.
Then something really scary happened.
Wanda's eyes glowed bright red!

I was sure the note was from her. Anyone
who could make their eyes glow could easily
zap a note onto my desk.

I was much too nervous to enjoy the rest of
show and smell. Ms. Vampira asked me if I
would like to bring something in next Thurs-

day. I said yes. I figured I could bring in some of Great-Uncle Dracula's frog soup.

After show and smell, it was time for math. The class was learning multiplication tables. In Plainville our math problems were about things like apples and oranges. The math problems that Ms. Vampira handed out were about tarantulas and snakes. I guess even math was different in Transylvania.

Finally the lunch bell rang. Ms. Vampira told everyone to line up in front of the room.

"Want to eat lunch with me?" Winnie whispered as we got in line. "I usually sit with Wolfie Johnson and Hector Specter."

I had to think for a moment. I wasn't sure that I wanted to eat lunch with a werewolf. What if he got hungry and took a bite out of me? I glanced over at Wolfie. He looked almost like a big puppy. How bad could a puppy be?

"Okay," I said.

The lunchroom in Transylvania Elementary did not look anything like the lunchroom at my old school. In Plainville the lunchroom was bright and sunny. There were pictures of different kinds of food hanging on the walls. Mrs. Wilson, the lunch lady, always wore a clean white apron. I liked the lunchroom at Plainville.

The lunchroom in Transylvania was very dark. There were cobwebs everywhere. The tables were big gray rocks. And the lunch lady was not wearing a white apron. She had on a long black dress like Ms. Vampira's. She was stirring something in a huge black pot.

Winnie, Wolfie, Hector, and I sat down at one of the big rock tables.

"Did you bring your lunch today, Emily?" Winnie asked.

Great-Uncle Dracula had packed lunches for me and Elliot that morning. "Yes, I did," I said. "But I'm not sure I'm going to like it. My great-uncle Dracula made it for me. He has very strange ideas about food."

"What do you mean?" Wolfie asked.

"Well, this morning he served frog soup for breakfast," I said.

"I love frog soup," said Wolfie.

"So do I," said Hector.

"Me too," said Winnie.

I felt pretty silly. I should have known that frog soup was popular in Transylvania.

"Well, let's see what Great-Uncle Dracula gave me for lunch," I said. I opened my brown paper bag. Inside there was a sandwich. At least I *thought* it was a sandwich. There were two pieces of bread with something black in between. It looked like bat wings were sticking out the sides.

"Oh, boy, bat wings on rye!" Hector said. "My favorite! Want to trade?"

I had no idea what ghosts ate for lunch, but anything would be better than bat wings. "What do you have?" I asked.

"Scream cheese and jelly," Hector said with a shrug. He handed me his sandwich. It looked like a regular cream cheese and jelly sandwich.

"Why do you call it scream cheese?" I asked.

"Because it screams when you take the bread off the top," Hector explained. "Like this." He lifted up the top slice of bread.

*"Aieee!"* screamed the sandwich.

I wasn't sure that I wanted to eat a screaming sandwich, but I was very hungry. I decided to take one very small bite.

The sandwich did not scream when I bit into it. And it was delicious. It tasted just like a normal cream cheese and jelly sandwich. I decided to ask Great-Uncle Dracula to make me a scream cheese and jelly sandwich for lunch every day.

As I ate my sandwich, I looked around the lunchroom. It seemed like the whole school was there. Across the room I could see Elliot. He was sitting at a table with about ten boys. Most of them looked like little vampires and werewolves. As usual, Elliot was laughing. He looked like he was having a great time.

Suddenly the room got very quiet. Winnie poked me in the arm.

"It's Principal Frank N. Stein," she whispered.

A very tall, skinny man had walked into the lunchroom. He was wearing a white coat like a doctor's and little round glasses. He also had white hair that stood straight up on top of his head.

Principal Stein got a big plate of food from the lunch lady and walked toward the teachers' room. Wanda stepped right in front of him.

"Principal Stein, I've been practicing very hard for the gross face contest," she said.

"That's very good, Wanda. I'm sure everyone is practicing hard," the principal said. Then he walked away.

Wolfie rolled his eyes. "Oh, brother," he said.

"What were they talking about?" I asked. "I've never heard of a gross face contest, but I saw a poster for one."

"Oh, it's the creepiest," Winnie said. "Every year the school has a big contest to see who can make the grossest face. There's a winner in every grade. This year's contest is going to be held on Monday."

"The winner gets a truly terrifying ten-foot trophy. It's a great honor," added Hector. "Wanda won last year."

"Wanda wins *every* year," said Wolfie.

"Really?" I said.

Winnie sighed. "Wanda is the best witch in the whole third grade. She thinks she's so great, but she's not very nice."

I looked over at the next lunch table. All the other witches in the third grade were sitting there with Wanda. Even some older kids were there.

"She looks pretty popular," I said.

"A lot of people want to be Wanda's friend. But that's only because they don't want her for an enemy," Winnie said. "If Wanda doesn't like you, watch out. She can be really mean."

Just then Wanda walked up to our table. She smiled sweetly. "Were you talking about me?" she asked.

"N-no, Wanda," Hector stammered. "We were just talking about the gross face contest."

"Why bother? Everyone knows I'm going to win," Wanda said. "Of course, it'll be fun to see Emily Weirdo here try to make a gross face. I'll bet she's never made a gross face in her life."

All the witches at Wanda's table heard her and cackled loudly.

I felt like crawling under the table. But the worst part was that Wanda was right. I'd never made a gross face before.

"Does everyone have to enter the contest?" I asked when Wanda walked away.

"Of course, silly," Winnie said. "But don't worry. You'll do fine."

I didn't say anything. How could I get up in front of the whole school and try to make a gross face? I wasn't a witch, a werewolf, a vampire, or a ghost. Wanda already thought I was a weirdo. Soon the whole school would think so too.

# ·4·

# A Town Full of Monsters

When the next bell rang, everyone marched back to their classrooms.

I was scared that Wanda would say something mean again during class, but she didn't. Even so, I was very glad when the last bell rang. As we were lining up to go outside, Ms. Vampira told the class that we'd have a spelling test the next day.

That made me feel a lot better. I am very good at spelling. Last year I got a hundred on almost every spelling test. At least there's one thing I don't have to worry about, I thought as we all walked outside.

There were lots of long black cars waiting in front of the school. I knew Great-Uncle Dracula was waiting for me in one of them. But which one? All the cars looked the same.

Then a small red head poked out of one of the car's windows. It was Elliot.

"Hey, Emily! Over here!" he shouted.

"Yes, Emily. You'd better hurry up and leave," said a voice behind me. It was Wanda, of course. "As a matter of fact," she added, "why don't you leave Transylvania? Go back to Plainville, where you belong."

I didn't know what to say. Why was Wanda picking on me like this?

Luckily Winnie, Wolfie, and Hector overheard.

"Why don't you leave Emily alone, Wanda?" said Wolfie.

Wanda looked at her friends. "It figures that a wimpy werewolf would make friends with a weirdo," she said. Then she smiled. "Say, Wolfie, I bet your aunt Moonerva would really be upset if something happened to her Putrid Perfume, wouldn't she?"

"What do you mean?" Wolfie asked.

"Oh, nothing," Wanda said. She started to walk away.

Suddenly Hector pointed at Wolfie's knapsack. "Oh, no!" he cried.

Wolfie's bottle of Putrid Perfume was floating out of his knapsack! But before any of us could grab it, the bottle crashed onto the sidewalk. Putrid Perfume spilled everywhere!

I had to hold my nose again. I couldn't help it.

"That Wanda is a rotten witch," Winnie said.

Even though I hated Putrid Perfume, I felt bad for Wolfie. "It's all my fault." I said. "None of this would have happened if I hadn't moved to Transylvania."

"Don't say that!" said Winnie. "We're glad you came to Transylvania."

I wasn't sure that *I* was glad. But Winnie, Wolfie, and Hector were being really nice.

"Thanks. I'm sure I'll love it here," I lied.

"Emily!" Elliot was screaming louder than a scream cheese sandwich.

I waved good-bye to my new friends and climbed into the front seat of Great-Uncle Dracula's car.

"So how was your first day at Transylvania Elementary?" Great-Uncle Dracula asked. He smiled at me and Elliot. He had very long white teeth.

"Great!" said Elliot.

I should have known that Elliot would fit right in at Transylvania Elementary. He was creepier than any monster I had met today.

"How about you, Emily?" Great-Uncle Dracula asked.

I decided I would be honest with him. Maybe Great-Uncle Dracula could help me figure out what was wrong with this place.

"I had a very strange day today," I told him. "I think everyone was playing some kind of a joke on me."

"A joke? What do you mean?" he asked.

"Well, they were all pretending to be witches and ghosts and werewolves," I said. "Even my teacher was dressed like a vampire."

"*My* teacher is a witch," said Elliot.

"Elliot, I am trying to talk to Great-Uncle Dracula. My teacher is crazy. Your teacher must be crazy too," I said.

Great-Uncle Dracula got a very serious look on his face. "Ms. Vampira is not crazy," he said. "She comes from one of the oldest vampire families in Transylvania."

"But vampires aren't real," I said. "You only see them in scary movies."

"Of course vampires are real," Great-Uncle

Dracula said. He pulled the black car into our driveway. *"I* am a vampire. And I am real."

Elliot was very excited now. "Our uncle's a real live vampire? Neat! I want to be a vampire too!" he said.

I didn't know what to think anymore. My own great-uncle wouldn't lie to me, would he? I thought about all of the mean things Wanda had done that day. No ordinary person could have done them. It looked like Transylvania, U.S.A., really was a town full of monsters!

Elliot tugged on the sleeve of my button-down sweater. "Hey, Emily, want to play in the backyard with me?" he asked. We had brought our swing set from Plainville to Great-Uncle Dracula's house.

Most of the time Elliot is a pest. I don't play with him much. But today I said yes.

We ran into the backyard and threw our books down on the grass. We played on the swings for a while. Then Elliot got a funny look in his eyes.

"Hey, Emily," he said. "Can you help me climb up to the top bar?"

"You know we're not allowed to do that, Elliot," I said.

"But I want to hang upside down like a vampire bat," Elliot said. "I need all the practice I can get."

That was the last straw. Was *everyone* around me going crazy?

"There are enough monsters in this town already!" I yelled, and stomped toward the house.

# ·5·

# No Garlic Bread Allowed

"Where's Dad?" I asked Great-Uncle Dracula as soon as I was inside.

"He is working on his book," Great-Uncle Dracula said.

I knew never to bother Dad while he was writing. There was nothing to do but wait.

Great-Uncle Dracula yawned. "I think I'll have a nap downstairs," he said.

"In the basement?" I said.

"Why, yes," he said. "That is where I sleep. Vampires need a dark place to nap in during the day."

"Oh," I said. I felt a little creepy. Did Great-Uncle Dracula sleep in a coffin, like the movie vampires? I decided I didn't want to find out.

Elliot stormed in from the backyard. "I'm going to have vampire practice in my room— *by myself!*" he yelled.

I didn't feel like answering him.

Instead, I sat down on Great-Uncle Dracula's dusty old couch and started studying for my spelling test.

After a long, long time, my dad came downstairs. His hair was messy, as usual. But he was smiling. It was very good to see him. Elliot and Great-Uncle Dracula came into the living room, too.

"Emily! Elliot!" Dad said. "How are you? I had a wonderful day. I wrote three chapters of my new book. I hope you two had a good time at school."

"I did!" said Elliot.

Then Dad looked at me. He's always telling me to say what's on my mind. So I did.

"I had a terrible day, Dad," I said.

Dad looked worried. "Why don't we talk

about this in the kitchen, Emily?" he said. "You can help me fix dinner."

Usually I like to help fix dinner. But today was not a usual day.

"What are we having?" I asked. "Spider casserole? Lizard lasagna?"

"Hey, Emily, what's gotten into you?" Dad said. He looked a little angry now. "We're having your favorite meal. Spaghetti with tomato sauce. And garlic bread."

"Garlic bread!" Great-Uncle Dracula gasped.

"Oh, my. Of course not, Uncle Drac. How could I forget?" Dad said. "I'm really sorry."

"What's wrong with garlic bread?" I asked.

"Uncle Dracula is er—allergic to garlic," Dad said.

"I'm allergic to garlic too," Elliot said quickly.

"Elliot, you are not allergic to garlic. You eat garlic bread all the time," I said.

"Not anymore. I want to be a vampire, just like Uncle Drac," Elliot said. "And if vampires are allergic to garlic, then so am I."

I couldn't take this anymore.

"My own brother is as crazy as everyone else in this town!" I screamed.

Dad, Great-Uncle Dracula, and Elliot stared at me. I am usually a quiet person. I guess they had never heard me scream before.

"Emily, I think we should have that talk now," Dad said.

Great-Uncle Dracula took Elliot upstairs so we could be alone.

Dad and I started to make the spaghetti. I told him everything that had happened to me that day. I told him about the scary note from Wanda and how her eyes glowed red. I told my dad how she used magic to break Wolfie's perfume bottle. And then I told him about the gross face contest.

Dad explained to me that things *were* different in Transylvania. He said that everyone really *was* a witch, a werewolf, a ghost, or a vampire. But he also said that they weren't really scary or dangerous, like in the movies.

"But what about Wanda, Dad?" I asked. "She's really mean."

"There are bullies in every school, Emily," Dad said. "Wanda will soon get bored with being mean to you. Besides, it sounds like you have three good friends already."

"I guess you're right, Dad," I said. But I still had one more question.

"Is Great-Uncle Dracula really a vampire?"

"Yes, he is, Emily," my dad answered. "But there's no reason to be afraid of him. He's as harmless as a—"

"Bat," Great-Uncle Dracula finished as he came into the kitchen. "And if you are lucky, I may change into one for you sometime."

"Can you really do that?" I asked.

"But of course," he said. "It is quite simple." Dad was pouring the tomato sauce on top of the spaghetti. "That smells delicious," Great-Uncle Dracula said.

"Vampires like spaghetti?" I asked.

"Oh, yes," he said. "We like the color of the sauce—blood red." Then he laughed.

I laughed too, but I still felt a little creepy. I'd have to get used to having a vampire for an uncle.

# ·6·

# The Spelling Test

The next day started out really well. Breakfast was a lot better. Great-Uncle Dracula made toast just for me. He even packed me a special scream cheese and jelly sandwich for lunch. And another good thing happened before school. Winnie was in line waiting for me. She looked happy.

"Emily, guess what?" she said. "It's my birthday tomorrow. Everyone in Ms. Vampira's class is invited to my party. Will you come too?"

"Sure!" I said. I love birthday parties. "Thanks, Winnie. That'll be fun."

Even school was okay that morning. We learned about gravity in science. Ms. Vampira explained how witches' brooms fly. It was very interesting.

Lunch was all right, too. I sat with Winnie and Wolfie and Hector again. My scream cheese and jelly sandwich was delicious. And so far Wanda hadn't said one mean thing to me!

After lunch, we had recess. Winnie and I played hopscotch on the playground. It was fun. But soon it was time to go back to class.

That's when things got bad.

Ms. Vampira told us it was time for the spelling test. Like I said before, I wasn't worried about it. But I should have known that even spelling tests were different in Transylvania.

Ms. Vampira asked who would like to go first.

Wanda raised her hand high. "I would, Ms. Vampira," she said.

"All right, Wanda. Please spell 'lizard' for us," said Ms. Vampira.

"That's easy," Wanda said. She closed her eyes tight. Then, instead of spelling the letters out, she said a poem:

"Blizzard, gizzard.
Let's have a lizard!"

There was a small puff of smoke. A tiny lizard appeared on Wanda's desk.

"Very good, Wanda," said Ms. Vampira. Then our teacher blinked her eyes, and the lizard disappeared.

Suddenly it dawned on me. This was not a test for spelling words. This was a test for *magic* spells! I didn't know any magic spells. I was in big trouble.

Ms. Vampira called on Winnie next. Her word was "bat."

Winnie closed her eyes just like Wanda had done. She said a little poem too:

"Drat, scat.
Show us a bat!"

There was another puff of smoke. But no bat showed up on Winnie's desk. Instead there

was a butterfly! That was fine with me. I like butterflies much better than bats. But Winnie looked sad.

"I'm sorry, Ms. Vampira," she said.

"That's all right, Winnie. This was much better than last time," Ms. Vampira said.

"I'll say," said Wanda loudly. "Last time she spelled up a stick of butter. At least a butterfly has wings."

"Wanda, please do not talk out of turn," Ms. Vampira said. Then she looked at me. "Emily, how about you? Can you spell 'spider'?"

I thought about closing my eyes like Winnie and Wanda. If I was really lucky, maybe a spider would appear. But I knew I'd just look silly. I had to tell Ms. Vampira the truth.

I looked down at my desk. "Well, no, I can't, Ms. Vampira," I said. "I'm just a regular person. I've never performed a magic spell in my life."

Some of the kids in the class gasped. I guess they were surprised.

"Oh, Emily, I'm so sorry," Ms. Vampira said. "I forgot. I'll think of some other way you can earn your grade."

"That's not fair, Ms. Vampira," Wanda called out. "Why should Emily get special treatment?"

"Because Emily is different, Wanda. Now, I won't have you talking out of turn again."

I raised my hand. "Ms. Vampira, I can spell spider the regular way. S-p-i-d-e-r."

Ms. Vampira smiled. "That's correct, Emily. Thank you."

Ms. Vampira continued to give the spelling test. I wasn't surprised when another note appeared on my desk a few minutes later. This one said: DON'T GO TO WINNIE'S PARTY IF YOU KNOW WHAT'S GOOD FOR YOU, EMILY *WEIRDO*.

This time I *knew* the note was from Wanda.

Winnie saw the note on my desk. She leaned over and whispered, "Don't listen to Wanda, Emily. It's my party, and I want you to be there. We'll have a great time tomorrow."

I wasn't so sure.

## ·7·

# Creepy Birthday to You

The next day was Saturday. I was very nervous about going to Winnie's party. It's no fun knowing that a real live witch is out to get you. But Great-Uncle Dracula said I would have a wonderful time.

Before the party, he took me to the Transylvania Shopping Mall. I needed to find a present for Winnie.

We went to a store called Witch World. I picked out a really neat hair clip shaped like a bat. It was black with two shiny red stones for eyes. I thought Winnie would like it. The saleswitch said it was their most popular item.

Then it was time to drive to Winnie's house. I was still nervous. Before I got out of the car, Great-Uncle Dracula kissed me on the cheek.

"Do not worry, Emily," he said. "I am sure everything will go well. If that Wanda gives you any trouble, just tell Winnie's mother."

"Okay," I said. But inside I was thinking, Only babies do that. Telling on Wanda would be the worst thing I could do. Then I got out of the car, and Great-Uncle Dracula drove off.

I walked up to the Witchersons' house and rang the doorbell. Winnie answered it. She was wearing a paper witch hat today. There were silver moons and stars all over it.

"Hi, Emily! Come on in," she said. She gave me a hat just like hers. I put it on.

"Here's your present, Winnie," I said.

"Thanks," Winnie said. "Why don't you put it on the dining room table?"

Winnie's dining room was crowded. Just about everyone in Ms. Vampira's class was there. I waved to Wolfie and Hector. Wanda was nowhere in sight. I felt relieved. Maybe she got sick, I thought. But then I heard a loud cackle. Wanda was standing in a dark corner of the room, surrounded by three other witches.

"Hey, it's Emily Weirdo!" she called.

My hands got very sweaty.

"Just ignore Wanda," Winnie said. "I have to help my mom in the kitchen, but I'll be right back."

I looked around the room. It was decorated with black balloons and black and orange streamers. There was a big long table piled with presents. All of the presents were exactly the same size and shape as mine. In the center of the table was a huge birthday cake. CREEPY BIRTHDAY TO YOU was written on it in black icing. It was at least ten layers high. There were candles all over it. It looked delicious. I couldn't wait to try some.

But first it was time to play a game. Winnie's mother came into the room. She had curly brown hair like Winnie. She was holding a big cardboard box. First she pulled a giant cardboard rat out of the box and tacked it on one wall. Then she brought out a blindfold, some tape, and what looked like a lot of paper rat tails.

"Who wants to play pin the tail on the rat?" she asked.

I figured that pin the tail on the rat must be like pin the tail on the donkey. So I raised my hand along with everyone else.

Hector went first. Mrs. Witcherson put the blindfold on him. Then she spun him around and around. He got so dizzy that he floated up to the ceiling! He pinned his tail up there.

A few other kids followed. They all missed the rat. Somebody even pinned Wolfie, but he said it didn't hurt. Then it was my turn.

Mrs. Witcherson blindfolded me. I heard Wanda whisper, "Let's have some fun with Emily Weirdo!" That made me very nervous. I wanted to tell Mrs. Witcherson not to spin me, but it was too late. Before I knew it, I was spinning around and around. I felt very dizzy. But that wasn't the worst part.

The first thing I remember is trying to take a step. The next thing I remember is sliding across the floor. And the last thing I remember is a big *squish*!

Even though I couldn't see, I knew what
had happened. I had landed right on top of
Winnie's birthday cake!

# ·8·

# The Meanest Girl in Transylvania

I took off my blindfold. Mrs. Witcherson was leaning over me.

"Are you hurt, Emily?" Mrs. Witcherson asked.

I didn't answer her right away. I was looking at a spot on the floor where a banana peel was quickly vanishing into thin air.

Then I heard someone laughing. It was Wanda. She had spelled up the banana peel that made me slip!

"The banana peel!" I yelled, pointing.

Winnie's mother gave me a strange look.

"What banana peel, Emily? I don't see a banana peel. Are you sure you're not hurt?"

"But—" I began. Then I realized Mrs. Witcherson would never believe me. The banana peel had disappeared. "No, Mrs. Witcherson," I said. "I'm okay."

Wanda pushed her way through the other kids and stuck her face close to mine. "You sure are clumsy, Emily Weirdo," she said. "Now we can't have any cake. You've ruined the whole party!"

"Emily didn't ruin the party," Winnie said. "I bet it's all *your* fault. You're up to your mean tricks again, aren't you, Wanda?"

Winnie's mother looked angry. "That's enough, Winnie," she said. "If you can't be polite to your guests, I'll have to send them home."

"Yes, Mom," Winnie said quietly. But she looked like she was going to cry.

The rest of the party was awful. Since I was covered with birthday cake, I had to go upstairs and clean up. Mrs. Witcherson put my dirty dress into a paper bag so I could bring it home. She gave me one of Winnie's witch dresses to wear.

While I was scrubbing myself off, I could hear the other kids downstairs. They were laughing and having a good time. Wanda was laughing loudest of all.

By the time I came downstairs, Great-Uncle Dracula was waiting to take me home. He was talking to Mrs. Witcherson. He looked very upset.

"I will call Wanda's mother as soon as I get home!" Great-Uncle Dracula was saying. "We will get to the bottom of this."

Oh, no, I thought. I hoped the other kids hadn't heard what Great-Uncle Dracula had just said. They already thought I was clumsy. I didn't want them to think I was a tattletale, too.

But I could already see Wanda glaring at me. She walked up and whispered in my ear. "If your crazy uncle rats on me," she said, "you're in big trouble on Monday." Then she walked away.

I gulped. Monday was the day of the gross

face contest. "Let's go home now, Great-Uncle Dracula," I said, tugging on his sleeve. "Everything's fine. Please don't call Wanda's mom."

Then I turned to Winnie. "Good-bye, Winnie," I said. "I'm sorry I ruined your party."

"You didn't ruin my party, Emily," Winnie said. But she still looked sad. I felt terrible.

I got into Great-Uncle Dracula's car. "I am sorry you didn't have a good time at the party, Emily," he said.

"It was okay," I said. I didn't feel like talking about it. Besides, I was kind of angry with Great-Uncle Dracula. I know he was just trying to help, but he'd made my problem with Wanda even worse.

I couldn't wait to get home. I wanted to talk to my dad again. But Great-Uncle Dracula said that Dad was working very hard. That night, he didn't even eat dinner with us. Great-Uncle Dracula brought a plate of food upstairs to him.

Next I tried to call my mom. Maybe she

could come and rescue me from this crazy place before the gross face contest on Monday. But all I got was her answering machine. The message said: "Hi. This is Mary Normal. I'm on a dig right now. Please leave a message and I'll call you when I get back."

Mom goes on digs all the time. She's an archaeologist. That means she goes to some place far away, like a desert or a mountain, and digs up rocks and bones. She says she's trying to learn about the history of the world.

I knew that my mom's work was very important. But I really needed to talk to her. I left a message that was not very nice: "Hi, Mom. This is Emily. Remember me? Call me when you're done digging up your stupid rocks."

Great-Uncle Dracula must have heard me leave that message. "Why, Emily," he said. "Is something wrong? You are certainly acting very strange."

"You think *I'm* strange?" I shouted. "I bet you think I'm a weirdo too!" Then I stomped up to my room and slammed the door.

When I woke up the next morning, I was hungry. I decided to go downstairs and get some breakfast. Dad was sitting at the table. He didn't look sleepy, and his hair was combed. There was a book in front of him.

"Come here, Emily," Dad said. "I have something to show you."

I sat down next to him, and I looked at the book. The words "Transylvania High School" were stamped on it in gold.

"This is my high school yearbook, Emily," my dad said. "Did you know that I grew up here in Transylvania?"

John Normal

Eve Witchy

"Really, Dad? Is *your* picture in here?" I asked.

"Yes, it is, Emily," he said. "I'll show you."

Dad turned the pages. I saw lots of pictures of teenage witches, werewolves, ghosts, and vampires. Then Dad stopped.

"Here I am," he said, pointing.

The guy in the picture didn't really look like Dad. His hair was very short. His ears stuck out. But the name underneath was John Normal. I guess it was him.

"Hey, Dad," I said. "You don't look like a werewolf or a vampire in this picture."

"Well, that's because I'm not, Emily," Dad said with a laugh.

"Oh," I said.

"My mom was born in Transylvania," Dad told me. "But my dad came from Plainville, just like you."

"Didn't everybody think you were strange?" I asked.

"Some people did, Emily. But my real friends didn't, and that's all that mattered," Dad said. "Now, why don't you tell me what's been bothering you?"

I told him all about how mad I was feeling inside. I told him about the mean trick Wanda played on me. And I told him about how scared I was to enter the gross face contest tomorrow. Everyone in third grade already thought I was a weirdo. Tomorrow the whole school would think so too.

Dad smiled. "Emily," he said, "we had a gross face contest every year when I was a student at Transylvania Elementary. I never won first place—but I still had fun. If I did it, you can do it too!"

That made me feel a little better. "I guess you're right, Dad," I said.

Just then Great-Uncle Dracula walked into the kitchen.

"Emily, something came for you in the mail yesterday," he said. He handed me a post-card.

I looked at it. There was a photo of a desert on the front. On the back was a handwritten message. It said: DEAR EMILY, I HOPE THINGS ARE GOING WELL IN TRANSYLVANIA. I MISS YOU VERY MUCH. CAN'T WAIT TO SEE YOU AGAIN. LOVE, MOM.

Things were definitely looking up.

# ·9·

# Three Jeers for Emily

When we got to school the next day, Elliot jumped out of the car.

"Bye, Uncle Drac," he said.

"Good-bye, Elliot. Good-bye, Emily," Great-Uncle Dracula said.

But I didn't want to leave just yet. I had something to say to my great-uncle.

"Great-Uncle Dracula, I'm really sorry," I said. "I've been so mean to you since we moved here. I guess I've just been nervous about fitting in."

"That is all right, Emily," he said. "I understand. Transylvania is not an easy place to get used to." He patted me on the shoulder. "Besides," he went on, "you should not worry so much about the contest."

"What do you mean?" I asked him.

Great-Uncle Dracula reached into his pocket. He pulled out a big tooth on a chain.

"What's that?" I asked.

"It is my magic wolf's tooth. I think it might help you at the gross face contest," Great-Uncle Dracula said. "After all, you do have some Dracula blood in you."

Great-Uncle Dracula placed the tooth in my hand. When I touched it, I could feel a little tingle. Could it really be magic?

"Thanks, Great-Uncle Dracula. It's the creepiest!" I said. I put the chain around my neck. "I guess I'd better go inside now."

"Just remember one thing, Emily," Great-Uncle Dracula said. "You are a very special person. Do not let anyone make you feel bad about yourself."

"I won't. And thanks!" I said.

Then it was time to face the kids in Ms. Vampira's class.

The first person I saw was Winnie. She was standing at the end of the third-grade line.

"Hi, Winnie," I said. "I'm sorry about your birthday cake. I guess the whole class thinks I'm a jerk."

"Are you batty, Emily?" Winnie asked. "Everyone knows that Wanda made you fall. Besides, we ate the cake anyway—it was only a little squished."

Just then a boy walked up to us. I didn't recognize him. He had curly dark hair and dark brown skin. And he was wearing regular blue jeans and a plain white button-down shirt.

"Hi," I said. "Are you new?"

The boy laughed. "Emily, it's me—Wolfie."

"Wolfie?" I said in surprise. "But—"

"I only look like a werewolf around the time when the moon is full," he said. "Most days I look pretty boring."

"Well, I think you look great," I told him.

Right then I didn't feel the least bit nervous about anything. Of course, that didn't last, because at that moment Wanda walked up to me.

"Just because your uncle didn't call my mom doesn't mean you're off the hook, Emily Weirdo," she said. "You're still going to lose the contest today."

For a second I was upset. But then I felt the wolf's tooth around my neck and remembered what Great-Uncle Dracula had said. I did have *some* Dracula blood in me.

"We'll see about that, Wanda," I said as the bell rang.

All morning the whole class was very excited. Ms. Vampira gave us another science lesson, but nobody learned much. The other kids were too busy fidgeting in their seats. I was too nervous to pay attention.

Finally the lunch bell rang, and we all headed for the lunchroom. There was a large platform set up at one end of it. Six ten-foot-tall trophies were lined up there. Each of them said: TO A TRULY TERRIFYING STUDENT OF TRANSYLVANIA ELEMENTARY SCHOOL.

Winnie told me that everyone would make their gross faces from up on the platform. Principal Stein and the teachers would sit in front of the platform and judge the contest. Each kid would be given a score: one point for not-so-gross, five points for really gross, and ten points for extremely gross. The person with the most points in each grade would win.

All the kids in the lunchroom were practicing for the contest. They were rolling their eyes and pulling their ears. I didn't practice. I did not even know where to begin. I just sat there and watched everybody else. There were a lot of gross faces being made all around me. I started to get nervous again.

Hector must have seen how scared I looked. "Don't worry," he said. "Remember, it's just for fun." That was what Dad had told me too.

Suddenly the room got very quiet. Principal Stein had just walked into the lunchroom. He stood on the platform and spoke into a tall microphone.

"Let the gross face contest begin!" he said. Everyone cheered. I had never felt so nervous in my life.

"First graders, please come to the platform," the principal said. Thirteen first graders, including Elliot, marched onto the platform.

"Let's see the first contestant, please," Principal Stein said.

A little werewolf stood by himself in the middle of the platform. He stuck his tongue way out. He rolled his eyes around and around. He certainly made a gross face.

A few other first graders followed. They all made gross faces. Soon it was Elliot's turn. He tried to make his eyes look in different directions. But he thought he was so funny that he just laughed and laughed. Nobody seemed to mind, though. Everyone gave him a big cheer.

When all the first graders had made their faces, the teachers handed their scorecards to Principal Stein. He started writing quickly on a piece of paper. Then he walked back to the microphone.

"Our first-grade winner is Greg Ghostmeister," the principal said. Everyone clapped. A little ghost walked up to the front of the platform. The principal handed him one of the giant trophies. It was three times bigger than he was! Still he managed to carry the trophy back to his seat.

Next it was the second graders' turn. By now I was much too nervous to watch the contest. Third grade would be next! I wasn't even paying attention when Principal Stein announced the second-grade winner.

Then I heard the awful words: "Third graders, please come to the platform."

I made sure I was last in line. Maybe there would be an earthquake. Then the contest would have to be canceled. But one by one the students in Ms. Vampira's class made their gross faces.

Wolfie tried his best werewolf sneer. But since he didn't look like a werewolf that day, he wasn't very convincing. Winnie whispered a little magic spell when it was her turn. But her face did not turn gross. A butterfly came out of her ear instead! It was a great trick, I thought. But it wasn't gross enough.

Hector made a very gross face. He made his eyes float right out of his head! It took him a few minutes to get them back, though.

Wanda made an even grosser face. She made every single hair on her head stand straight up. Then she stretched out her ears so they were about two feet long and wrapped them around her head. Everyone clapped very loudly for Wanda.

Before long, everyone in Ms. Vampira's class had made a gross face but me. I hoped no one would notice.

"Will the last contestant please make her face?" Principal Stein said.

I felt a little sick. My knees were shaking.

Slowly I walked to the middle of the platform. I had no idea what I was going to do.

But then I heard a voice behind me. It was Wanda.

"Let's see what you can do, Emily Weirdo!" she whispered loudly. "Not much, I bet."

I looked down at the wolf's tooth around my neck. Great-Uncle Dracula had said I was very special. Maybe he was right. I held the tooth in my hand, and I felt the tiny magic tingle again.

"Come on, Weirdo. Stop wasting time!" Wanda shouted.

Suddenly I was very tired of Wanda calling me names. I was tired of being called weirdo. And most of all I was tired of being afraid of a stupid kid witch.

The angrier I got, the more the wolf's tooth began to tingle. Suddenly my whole body started to tingle, too. My face got very hot, and my teeth felt like they were wiggling in my mouth. My eyes opened extra wide.

Before I knew what was happening, I heard myself scream, "I AM NOT A WEIRDO!"

The whole lunchroom got very quiet. Then everybody began to clap and scream and whistle! "Gross! Gross! Gross!" they shouted. They were *cheering* for me!

Principal Stein came onto the platform. He was holding a truly terrifying ten-foot trophy.

"Emily Normal," he said, "that was the grossest face anyone at Transylvania Elementary has ever seen!"

I couldn't believe it. Winnie came running up to me. "Three jeers for Emily!" she cried.

Everyone screamed again. I still couldn't believe it. "Did I really make a gross face?" I asked Winnie.

"Emily, it was amazing," she said. "Your skin turned purple. Your eyes popped out of your head. Your two front teeth became long white fangs. You made the grossest face of all time!"

"Thanks to Wanda," I said. I looked over and saw Wanda sulking all by herself at the back of the lunchroom. Then I touched the wolf's tooth again. "Great-Uncle Dracula helped me, too," I told Winnie. "And so did you and Hector and Wolfie. You guys are the best!"

"And you're the creepiest, Emily!" Winnie said.

At that moment I think I was the happiest girl in Transylvania.

## About the Author

*Great-Uncle Dracula* is JAYNE HARVEY's first book. She spends a lot of her time reading, watching scary movies, and searching for a real town like Transylvania. "I've met a few witches so far," she says, "but no vampires—yet!" Jayne Harvey lives outside New York City.

## About the Illustrator

"I've always loved scary books and scary movies," says ABBY CARTER, "so drawing the creepy characters in *Great-Uncle Dracula* was a lot of fun." Abby Carter is the talented illustrator of several books for children, including *Baseball Ballerina*. She lives in Cape Elizabeth, Maine, with her husband and daughter.

# Her Teeth Are Stones